This book belongs to

In honour of Belle, the scruffiest poodle of all,
and Scamp, my favourite street dog.

Special thanks to Harriet Birkinshaw for helping Monty to find Ginger,
and to Lilly Gottwald for making the book more beautiful than I'd hoped.

Text and illustrations © Katie Harnett 2019.
First edition published in 2019 by Flying Eye Books, an imprint
of Nobrow Ltd. 27 Westgate Street, London, E8 3RL.

Katie Harnett has asserted her right under the Copyright, Designs and
Patents Act, 1988, to be identified as the Author and Illustrator of this Work.

Published in the US by Nobrow (US) Inc.
Printed in Poland on FSC® certified paper.

1 3 5 7 9 10 8 6 4 2

ISBN: 978-1-911171-77-5
www.flyingeyebooks.com

MONTY

and the Poodles

BY KATIE HARNETT

FLYING EYE BOOKS

LONDON | NEW YORK

Monty lived on Green Street
on the north side of town.

Ginger lived in Poodle Mansions
on the south side of town.

But one day they saw each other at the gallery. . .

Monty had thought that poodles weren't friendly, but Ginger was very nice.
She showed him where she lived and told him all about the owner, Miss Lillabet.

Ginger had thought dogs like Monty were scary, but Monty was kind.

He took Ginger to all of his favourite places...

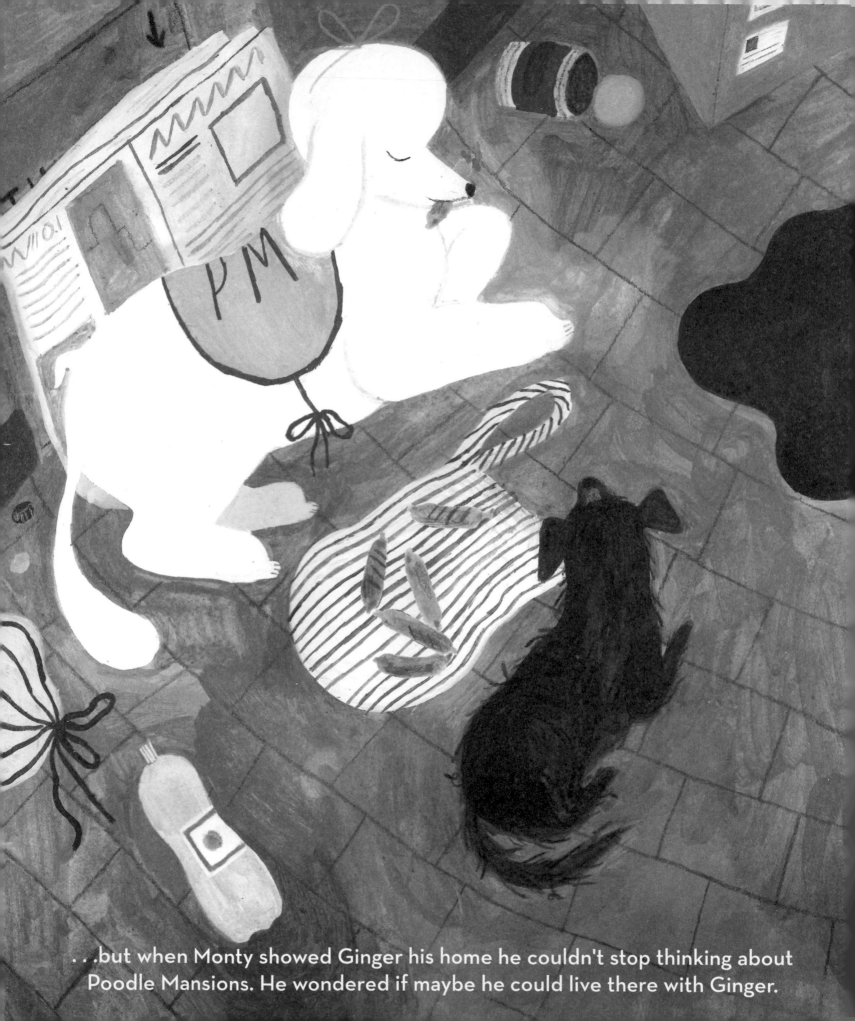

. . .but when Monty showed Ginger his home he couldn't stop thinking about Poodle Mansions. He wondered if maybe he could live there with Ginger.

Ginger thought this was a great idea...

. . .but Miss Lillabet was not pleased.

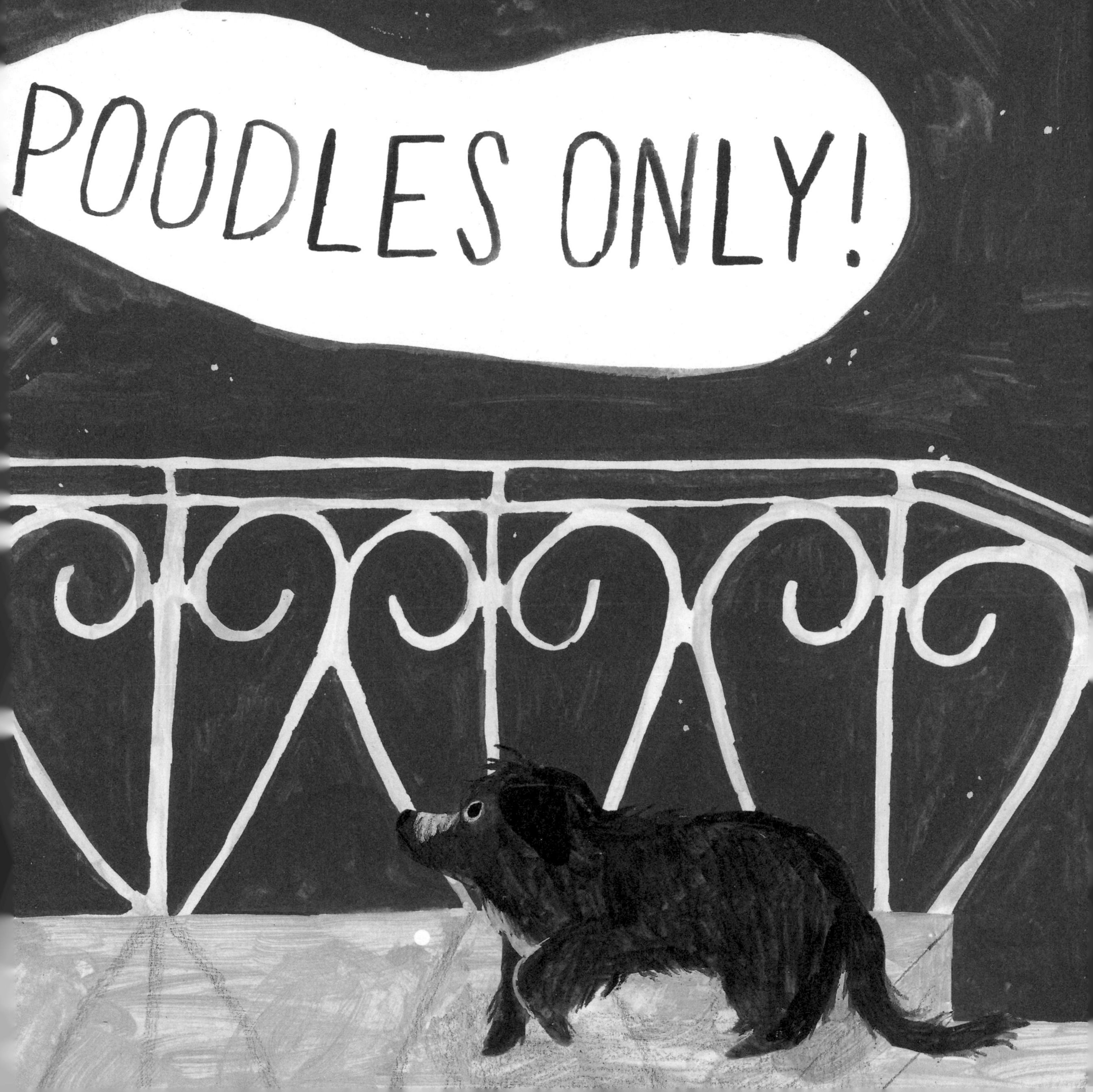

That night, Monty was the saddest he had ever been.

Ginger wasn't happy either. So she hatched a cunning plan.

Monty and the poodles crept and sneaked...

. . .and washed and fluffed until Monty looked just like a poodle!

Being a poodle was even better
than Monty could have ever imagined.

A POODLE NEVER
SPEAKS TO SCAMPS
AND MUTTS

A POODLE IS ALWAYS
NEAT AND TIDY

POODLES ARE SEEN
AND NOT HEARD

But life at Poodle Mansions was very tiring for Monty and
he didn't see why he should have to pretend anymore.

The poodles liked him just as he was.
So from now on, he was going to be himself!

It didn't go well.

Days later, Ginger still hadn't seen Monty.
Without him, Poodle Mansions didn't seem
like such a nice place to live after all.

is always composed
is always on time
never eats between meals
never runs
are seen & not heard
do NOT associate
Rules ~
CHORES
• Clean
• Tidy
• Washing
• Gardening

So Ginger and the poodles decided to find him.

They looked in all of Monty's favourite places.

They looked in all of *their* favourite places.

And finally, Ginger found him.

Monty was very surprised to see his friends!

And he had a big surprise for them too.

The cinema was old and drafty, but together

they could make it into a beautiful home. . .

...where everyone was welcome.